"He's Your Dog, Charlie Brown!"

"He's Your Dog,

Charlie Brown!"
by Charles M. Schulz

SCHOLASTIC BOOK SERVICES

NEW YORK · TORONTO · LONDON · AUCKLAND · SYDNEY · TOKYO

Copyright © 1968 by United Feature Syndicate, Inc. Produced in association with Lee Mendelson-Bill Melendez TV Production. Illustrations from the Lee Mendelson-Bill Melendez television production "He's Your Dog, Charlie Brown!" All rights reserved. This StarLine Edition is published by Scholastic Book Services, a division of Scholastic Magazines, Inc., by arrangement with The World Publishing Company.

30 29 28 27 26 25 24 23 22 21 20

7 8 9/7 01/8

"He's Your Dog, Charlie Brown!"

What do you do when everyone in the neighborhood is complaining about your dog?

Snoopy had certainly been acting up lately, and the kids were demanding that Charlie Brown do something about it.

"Why me?" he asked.

"Because he's your dog, Charlie Brown!"

That did it. Charlie Brown was forced into action, and he decided to write a letter to the Daisy Hill Puppy Farm.

DEAR DAISY HILL PUPPY FARM,
I AM WRITING IN REGARD
TO ONE OF YOUR LESS
DISTINGUISHED ALUMNI.

UNFORTUNATELY THIS
ALUMNUS IS NOT LIVING
UP TO MY EXPECTATIONS.
THEREFORE, I AM GOING TO
SEND HIM BACK AND HAVE YOU
TEACH HIM A LITTLE DISCIPLINE.

"This is for your own good, Snoopy, and don't look at me like that. You have no one to blame but yourself."

"Now, one other thing...I'm going to call Peppermint Patty and make arrangements for you to spend the first night at her house."

"Hello, Peppermint Patty? Hi, this is 'Chuck,' you know... 'Chuck' Brown...Yeah...Well, I have a favor to ask. Snoopy is going back to school for a few days and he needs a place to stay tonight. Yeah, it's too far to make it in one day. Can you put him up for the night?"

"Sure, Chuck... Glad to oblige."

Now, the weird thing about Peppermint Patty is that she somehow has never quite realized that Snoopy is a dog. She has always been impressed by Snoopy's baseball playing and her enthusiasm has sort of blinded her.

They said good-by and Snoopy set
off with his dog dish on his head
and carrying his little suitcase.
He was quite unhappy, a little
frightened, and very mad.

Snoopy was really not in much of
a hurry to get where he was going,
so he meandered

down a few side streets,

kicked some tin cans,

and just took his time.

When he finally got to Peppermint Patty's house, he was greeted warmly.

"Hi, Snoopy, ol' pal! How's the ol' shortstop? It's good to see you again. Come on in, and I'll show you your room."

After Snoopy unpacked, Peppermint Patty fixed him a little snack in the kitchen. She was surprised when she saw him put his whole nose in a bowl of cereal. "This is the strangest kid I've ever seen," she thought to herself. But that was only the beginning.

Now, Snoopy seated himself at a
little table out in her backyard
and really began to make a nuisance
of himself. He leaned back in his
chair and pretended that he was a
World War I flying ace on leave in

Paris, and he snapped his fingers
for service just as if he were in a
little sidewalk café. Peppermint
Patty was too polite to say anything
and she brought him a glass of
root beer.

This went on for three days.
Snoopy swam in the pool, sunned
himself in the yard, and snapped
his fingers whenever he wanted
something.

Peppermint Patty was getting a
little worried. The dishes in the
sink were beginning to pile up, and
she was getting tired of waiting
on this guest who was taking unfair
advantage of her good nature.
"I'll have to call Charlie Brown,"
she said to herself.

"Hello, Chuck? I don't know about this friend of yours here. He seems to think he's on vacation or something. I thought he was supposed to go to school."

"You mean he's still there?" cried Charlie Brown. "I'll be right over and get him!"

Charlie Brown grabbed a leash and set off across town. He hated the thought of putting a leash on Snoopy, but he could see no other way of controlling this dog who had gotten so out of hand.

And was Snoopy ever upset when
Charlie Brown snapped the leash
onto his collar and tried to drag
him home!

Snoopy put on a wild performance
pretending that the leash was
strangling him. He coughed and
he gasped, and he rolled on the
ground.

Finally, he leaped to his feet,
gave the leash a great yank so that

it flew from Charlie Brown's hand,
and ran back to Peppermint Patty's
house.

"You're back again? Well, look, friend," said Peppermint Patty, "I'll let you stay awhile longer because I sort of like you, but let's get one thing straight. Around this house, everyone has to do his share. That's a family rule. You can stay with us if you want. You're perfectly welcome, but you're going to have to work! Did you hear me? Work!"

And Snoopy worked.
Peppermint Patty had
him doing dishes...

mowing grass...

washing windows...

vacuuming rugs...

and taking out the trash.

It wasn't long before Snoopy
realized that he was caught between
the leash and more work than he ever
knew existed.

And when he got careless
and broke a dish, Peppermint

Patty banished him to the garage
for the night.

There's nothing worse than being
banished to the garage.

Snoopy felt terrible. It was

dark, and for the first time in his life, he knew what it was really like to be lonesome.

Fortunately, Peppermint Patty had not locked the door, so Snoopy was able to sneak out, go into the house, gather all his things together, and run for home.

When Charlie Brown saw Snoopy
at the front door, he threw his arms
in the air and grabbed him.

They danced around and around.
And when they went to bed, Charlie
Brown said, "It's good to have you
back, Snoopy."

Of course, they had to compromise
a little. Charlie Brown agreed not
to send Snoopy away and Snoopy
agreed to try to act a little less
outrageously.

The next day, Snoopy realized he had learned a good lesson.

"When it comes right down to it,"
he thought, as he stretched out
under the bright blue sky, "dogs
are born to sleep in the sun."